A day with the Animal Builders

Sharon Rentta

ALISON GREEN BOOKS

It's Donkey's first day at work. He's an Apprentice on a Building Site, and he's going to learn all about building houses.

The first thing Donkey learns is that you're not supposed to tread in the wet concrete. Oops.

All the animals have different jobs: spreading concrete, drilling and digging.

Snoozing isn't
a proper job.

These are some of the other builders. They all have Special Skills, and they're going to teach Donkey everything they know, which is a lot.

Apprentice

Digger
Operator

Electrician

Bricklayer

A Good All-Rounder

Foreman

Bert the Foreman is in charge. Everyone has to do what Bert says. Right now, Bert says it's time for a cup of tea and a biscuit.

Plumber

Carpenter

Drill
Operator

Scaffolder

Architect

Crane Operator

These are the builders' favourite types of biscuit:

Iced Cookie

Jammy Dodger

Chocolate
Biscuit

Dog Biscuit

Pink Wafer

The builders are building a house for the Penguin Family. It's going to be the penguins' Dream Home. The house is designed by an Architect. He decides what the house will look like, and where all the doors and windows will go.

The penguins say their house absolutely must have all these things:

Bedroom with Bunk Beds

Sandpit

Ice Rink

Really Big Fridge

Swimming Pool
on the Roof

Helter-Skelter

Toilets

Kitchen Sink

The Architect says it will be a Total
Headache fitting that lot into one house.

Donkey learns that there are lots of different stages to building a house:

1. Turtle and Yak clear the ground, and make it nice and flat.

2. The foundations come next. They go underneath the house. Frogs dig the trenches and Hippo fills them with concrete.

3. Next Beaver builds the walls on top of the foundations.

4. Llama, the carpenter, nails down the floorboards.

5. The ferrets normally tile the roof . . . but the penguins aren't having a roof. They're having a swimming pool instead.

7. The house needs wiring, so that it has electricity to make things work.

6. An Octopus is handy for putting in doors and windows.

8. It needs plumbing, so that it has running water.

9. Lizards plaster the walls, to make them look nice and smooth.

10. Hedgehogs paint and decorate . . . and the house is finished!

Donkey's keen to get cracking now. The first thing he's going to learn is Bricklaying, and Beaver's going to teach him.

Beaver says the key thing is to go carefully, carefully, and arrange the bricks in nice, neat rows.

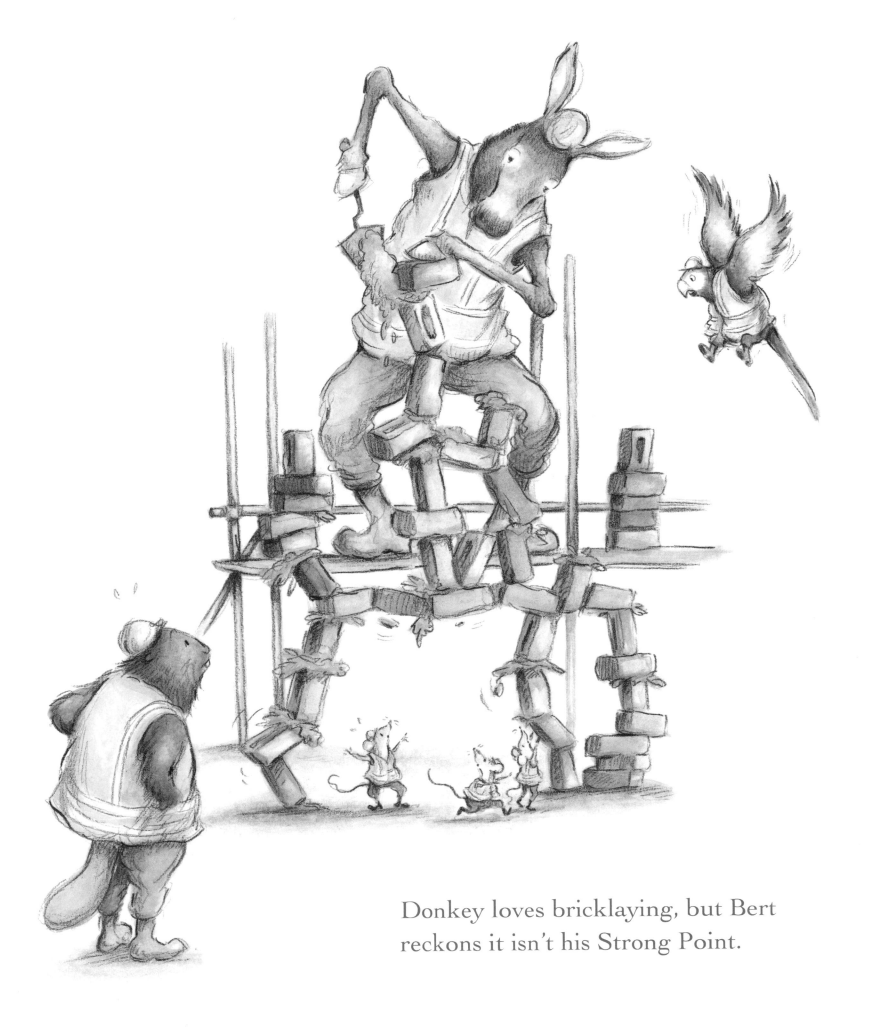

Donkey loves bricklaying, but Bert reckons it isn't his Strong Point.

Next Donkey gets to grips with some Heavy Machinery.
The Bulldozer is especially good fun. Donkey may not be
much good at building walls, but he's brilliant
at knocking them down.

SLAM!

Pity they didn't want him to.

It's amazing how much rubble comes out of a Dumper Truck.
Bert says Donkey's a Positive Danger behind the wheel.

It's time to put in the Plumbing.
They all find it a bit of a puzzle.

Building houses is hungry work.

The Crane is a good place to have lunch.

This is what the builders like for lunch:

Bones

Carrots

Sandwiches

Iced Buns

Worms

Builders' Tea

Fruit

From time to time, the penguin family
pop round to see how everything's going.
They've picked a bad moment for today's visit.

Bernard's got hooked on the crane.

Pig's fallen asleep in
the wheelbarrow.

ANIMALS
AT
WORK

And Donkey's got stuck in the concrete again. He has to be chipped out with a chisel.

Luckily, the penguins are very
happy with the Helter-Skelter,
which has just been finished.

Everyone tests it to make
sure it's working.

They check the Ice Rink's working, too.
The house is nearly finished!

But the very next day, Disaster strikes. When Turtle parked
the bulldozer, he forgot to put the handbrake on.

It starts rolling forwards and it's
going to smash into the house!

All the builders' hard work will be ruined.

But what's Donkey up to with that rope? He does his best cowboy impression – Yee-Hah! Then he swings the rope around like a lasso . . .

. . . and catches the runaway bulldozer just in time.

It's really heavy, but Donkey holds on tight, till Turtle clambers in and puts the brakes on. Phew! The house is saved!

At long last Donkey's discovered what his Strong Point is

– he's really, really strong!

Now Bert asks Donkey to do all the jobs
that require Extra Special Strength.

He carries all the bricks
they need to finish the house.

He removes the snoozing pig.

He heaves the Really Big Fridge off the lorry.

He carries in a few other things, too.

And he removes the snoozing pig again.

The house is finally ready. The penguins
invite the builders to join them for a
party in their brand new swimming pool.

And guess who makes the Biggest Splash?

Donkey does! Well done, Donkey!

That's another thing you're really good at!

For Builder Ben

First published in 2013 by Alison Green Books
An imprint of Scholastic Children's Books
Euston House, 24 Eversholt Street
London NW1 1DB
A division of Scholastic Ltd
www.scholastic.co.uk
London ~ New York ~ Toronto ~ Sydney ~ Auckland
Mexico City ~ New Delhi ~ Hong Kong

Copyright © 2013 Sharon Rentta

HB ISBN: 978 1 407134 87 1
PB ISBN: 978 1 407134 88 8